The Dis-condition of Ease

Owen Patterson

BREVIS Publishing ■ Chicago

The *Dis-condition of Ease* is a collection of prose fiction and short stories. These vignettes showcase everyday happenings in not so everyday ways. Easily relatable characters coupled with surprising twists of irony and suspense, make an entertaining reading experience. There is subtle comic flair that pleasantly balances the darker elements and themes. Throughout, the characters are shown to be intelligent; and with little effort or forethought, demonstrate honor, loyalty, and faith.

Titles by Owen Patterson

The Dis-condition of Ease (prose fiction, 2015)

Lovely Faze (poetry, 2017)

Stars at Naught (poetry, 2018)

Jaded (poetry, 2018)

Fear Naught
The Junk Drawer of Poetry (poetry/prose, 2019)

See online book reviews at *Windy City Reviews*

BREVIS Publishing
Chicago, IL USA
ISBN: 978-0-9964834-2-1
        978-1-5187363-4-6 (CS)
        978-0-9964834-0-7 (eBook)

Formatting by Owen Patterson; **2018 EDIT** x6-6.2
Cover design by "Pica"; Edmund Barca Gaylord

Special Thanks: Yasmeen Nazirah Patterson Ahmad, Michael Louis Ward, Lisa Richmond, Lamorris Richmond, Edmund Barca Gaylord

Thanks for your advice and help.

CONTENTS

INTRO (Poem)- *Persevere*

Rorschach 1

The Clown 5

Gideon's Shiva 11

¿Qué Milagro? What Miracle? 15

On To My Usual Place 21

To Be Acqainted 23

Wind and Tree 27

The Conditional Student 31

I'm Not Lazy, I Just Don't Do Yard Work 35

Lighthouse Beacon *(parts 1-3)* 41

You Bastard! 53

Heartland *(parts 1- 10)* 57

ADDENDUM

A Beautiful Night For A Sleepwalk...

With Sunsglasses 107

Gratitude 109

Break my bones

I crawl faster

Cleave my heart

I love twice

Stone my head

I know better

Rorschach

Thaddaeus Thomas, the resident junior class slacker, has once again been called to the office. He sits patiently, waiting to hear his name. His calm could easily be mistaken for indifference. Of course, it's not often so simple.

Brother Judah is the school counselor. He is a Christian Brother nearing the end of his tenure. His pure white beard and aching knees beg for retirement. But he has one last mission to complete.

Brother Judah opens the door to his office, "Thaddaeus, come in. Have a seat."

Thaddaeus walks in and smiles as he sits. He is very familiar with this space and with Brother Judah. He likes the aging brother.

"Thaddaeus..."

"Rorschach... I told you Brother, my friends call me Rorschach."

"I'm not going to call you Rorschach."

"Hmm, OK."

Brother Judah sits back in his chair and sighs. He knows this young man well and sees what others can't or won't. Thaddaeus hides his intellect and sensitivity so not to be vulnerable.

"Thaddaeus, you're failing or nearly failing every class. The administration is not going to let you waste your parents' money. They're going to put you out."

"They should do whatever they have to."

"Stop acting like you don't care. I know you do. You have a lot of potential. You're so smart."

Brother Judah may never know how much Thaddaeus appreciates these talks. He'll never know because Thaddaeus will never say. He doesn't speak in explicit terms. He speaks from the heart, but everything he says is like a riddle or ancient parable.

"Brother, don't misunderstand. OK, I can see how you *could* misunderstand." Thaddaeus pauses for a moment before continuing, "Brother, there's a reason my friends call me Rorschach. I'm not intelligent. I'm creative."

"Thaddaeus, you can be both."

"I'm a donkey's anus."

"What?" Brother Judah is accustomed to Thaddaeus' roundabout way of talking, but this surprises the veteran counselor. "What are you talking about?"

"All donkeys are asses, but not all asses are donkeys."

Brother Judah is speechless.

Thaddaeus continues, "Sometimes words have meaning. Sometimes they are just beauty. Sometimes you see a butterfly. Sometimes, it's just gum on pavement."

Brother Judah can't help but think that he has somehow failed his mission.

Thaddaeus can't help but think that he has succeeded in his.

The Clown

Jacob Segan Lévy left his home that evening without sitting for dinner. He simply needed some time. He was on a quest. Though, not knowing for what he searched, he wandered.

A man of simple means, Jacob dressed not to impress, but to blend. He was usually neat and casual. This night he wore pleated grey slacks, a pressed white shirt, and polished black leather shoes. A fairly ordinary man walked the streets.

Lost in thought, Jacob found himself on a street of artisan shops. He knew of the place, but had not ventured there. He knew little of arts and crafts, but was curious.

Jacob came upon one shop that from the outside appeared not dissimilar to the others. But when he peered inside, he saw that it was an art gallery. His gaze was immediately captured by an absurd painting in the farthest corner. Jacob entered the gallery and gave not even the slightest glance to the other canvasses. He headed directly for that absurd painting in the rear.

Jacob stared fixedly at that absurd painting. A woman, at least half Jacob's age, gingerly approached. She stood beside him. She was clearly young and clearly attractive, but dressed well beyond her years. She was downright frumpy. She wore a collarless long-sleeved white blouse, buttoned to the top. Her ankle length skirt was dark brown and pleated. Her flats were plain brown. The two of them, side by side, could have been framed and placed on a gallery wall.

Jacob did not notice her.

The young woman observed Jacob making faces at the painting. He jutted his head forward and back again. He tilted his head far to the right, and then to the left. Anyone might have wondered at his sanity. Anyone might have inquired as to his intent. The young woman merely asked, "Do you like it?"

Without looking at her he responded, "I don't know about art. This painting confuses me." Jacob did not answer her question. She thought it to be odd, but was still intrigued.

"Why is this painting the only one that you've looked at?"

"I told my wife that I was going out to find someone to have sex with."

Again, she found his response odd. "That's cruel!" she said.

"Well, tit for tat."

"Did you really say that to your wife?"

"Well, no, not really."

"You are a *real* clown."

Jacob did not respond to her comment. He began to ponder aloud about the absurd painting. The setting was a park with green grass, trees, and colorful flowers. There was a clown performing. His audience was just a few feet away. The clown stood on his left leg with his right leg lifted and bent at the knee. On his right foot, he balanced a stick with a spinning plate. On his knee was perched a parrot. The clown wore a cap made from a burlap sack. Atop the cap, sat a tiny Chihuahua. The clown did all of this while juggling three red balls.

The clown's head was slightly tilted to the right. He smiled, but it wasn't real. It was a false half smile.

His eyebrows were raised high into his forehead and his eyes were sad.

The audience, on the other hand, was hysterical with laughter.

The boys wore little sailor suits. The girls wore ankle length dresses tied at the waists with ribbons. They wore brimmed straw hats with flowers. Little fingers pointed. Their heads flung back with mouths agape. Men in suits, vests, and derby hats, clutched their fat bellies. The women, in their lovely dresses, fancy hats, and with tiny parasols, were doubled over in some exquisite joy. All eyes were tightly shut and tearing. None were actually looking at the clown. The artist's depiction was so impressive, that Jacob could actually hear the exuberant laughter.

The clown's face was the source of Jacob's confusion. The false half smile was needy and appeared to ask, "Am I entertaining?" While the sad eyes asked, "Are you laughing at me?"

The young woman heard all of Jacob's musings and ruminations, and finally said, "You relate to this painting. Are *you* a *real* clown?"

Jacob turned to her for the first time and said, "Ah, I get it now. All that he is doing, they should be clapping, not laughing. He feels unappreciated." Jacob then contorted his face into a false half smile, arched his eyebrows high into his forehead, and projected sad eyes. The young woman was startled because Jacob had so completely morphed into the clown. She feared Jacob's obsession.

Jacob finally relaxed his face and said, "I'm not a clown. I'm an old-school parent. My children are very modern. And my wife dreams of something different; something not me."

Jacob said nothing more. He turned and walked away.

Exiting the gallery, Jacob gave not even the slightest glance to any other canvass. Walking down the street, he heard the young woman call to him, "Please, come again!"

Jacob Segan Lévy approached his small but comfortable home. He thought to himself, as always, "Maybe, it'll be different this time."

Gideon's Shiva

Gideon wakes.

Gideon, the "Great Warrior" from the Book of Judges... How does one live up to a name?

Gideon sits up in his bed. He was never a genius, but he always had an ability to see beauty and color in the lesser of places. Though today renders him color-blind, or at least color diminished. He wonders at the ailment.

Light weighs in through the large parlor windows. The light is sluggish, and lacks luster. The colors of his world are now muted. He walks through a gray house that was once filled with beautiful things. The art remains, but the hues have faded. The walls appear as dark cloth.

Gideon sits in the parlor and looks out into the world panoramic. He realizes that the world has changed. Some great calamity befalls humanity. The world's light filters through dust and ash. He wonders if all the forests are ablaze. Have all the mountains erupted, spewing caustic clouds?

Gideon notices people gathered in rooms, seeking shelter from the tragedy. He feels content. His family and friends are safe in his home. Yet, no one speaks as Gideon walks through. No one notices except one small child. The boy smiles and quickly returns to mundane distractions; action figures and sweet treats.

Pacing back and forth by the bathroom door, is Chen; the underappreciated younger brother of Gideon's boss. Chen's expression is of anguish. As always, Gideon is empathetic and says in a soft voice, "It's OK. I'm waiting too." Chen stops and looks toward Gideon, but says nothing. His expression is not less agonized. Chen, is so sad.

Gideon leaves his friend and returns to the parlor. There are candles. Thoughts turn to an old flame. "Is she alright? Is she safe?"

Gideon picks up the phone and dials. A male voice answers, but the connection is poor. The voice says, "Hello! Hello! Hello!" Gideon yells back as loud as is possible. The male voice finally responds, "Yes! She's here! But asleep!" The line goes dead. Gideon more than hears the click, he feels the disconnection.

Light outside becomes intermittent. Gideon remembers days when he was young. Thick white clouds would roll across the sky, casting colossal shadows on God's Land. Rays of light fell between the clouds, dotting the countryside like Morse code. Dots and dashes, offered perhaps a message from heaven.

Gideon emerges from his reminiscence and sees that the world has changed yet again. A great storm manifests. A wall of white replaces the dusky yellow light. Only then does Gideon look down and notices his wedding band. The yellow of the gold contrasts the gray of everything. The band shines. The band is brilliant. But it's not right. It's not on his ring finger. It lies in the palm. It falls away. It disappears; obscured by endless gray. The color lingers in thought. Memory is kindled and preserved. He longs for her.

The white is not cold like snow. It is not hot like the sun's core. Gideon feels peace. He steps into the white and leaves the dark cloth and gray walls behind.

Color returns, and is endless.

¿Qué Milagro?

What Miracle?

What can be said about Tomás? He is a pessimist. The most central and fixed characteristic of his life, is his self-loathing. His negative attitude festers like an infectious boil that threatens to explode at any time, perverting the world around him. In spite of this, Tomás works miracles. He transforms thought into reality. It is *not very* obvious, but Tomás is a saint. He is a saint not for the deeds themselves, but for the power to transform. Everything that he touches, turns to shit. What a miracle! If he were a farmer, his soil would be so rich. But in life, it is not to be. His wealth begins now, at his end.

Says the priest:

His twisted body is healthy. His tortured mind, knows peace. His broken heart is repaired. He is in the arms of God. His doubt is proven false. It is a testament of his transformation, that so many have come today. He *was* alone. In heaven, he mingles with the hosts of angels. What a miracle, that he instructs us even now, by his twisted life. Like they say in English, "Every cloud has a silver lining."

At this exact moment, a dark and ominous cloud appears in the sky. It moves slowly, but determined. It crosses the sky, threatening to cover the entire world. What great power he demonstrates, even in death! What a miracle!

Meanwhile, on the other side of the pueblo...

What can be said about Angélica? She is an optimist. The most central and fixed characteristic of her life, is her high self-esteem. Her positive attitude blossoms in the Rose-garden of Eden. A flowery sun rises in the sky to beautify the world. In this light, she works miracles. She transforms thought into reality. It is *very* obvious that Angélica is a saint. She is a saint for her good deeds as much as for the power to transform. Everything that she touches, becomes a good harvest. People say that where Angélica walks in the fields, the corn grows very tall and very sweet. In her footsteps are found singular rosebuds without thorns. What a miracle! If she were a farmer, her yield would be so rich. But in life, it is not to be. She only thinks of others. Her wealth begins now, at her end.

Says the priest:

Her fine body adds to the beauty of paradise. Her altruistic mind is rewarded. Her pure heart lives within that of God. It is sad that we are separated from our Angélica. But we are consoled that she is in the arms of God. Her faith is proven true. It is a testament of her grace, that so many have come today. In heaven, she mingles with the hosts of saints. What a miracle, that she instructs us even now, by her sacred life. Although, she is no longer with us, I believe that she watches over us. Like they say in English, "Every cloud has a silver lining."

At this exact moment, a dark and ominous cloud appears in the sky. It moves slowly, but determined. It crosses the sky, threatening to cover the entire world. What great power she demonstrates, even in death! What a miracle!

Tomás and Angélica were worlds apart while living in the same little pueblo. Fate can be ironic. Whatever one's station, Death, is the Great Equalizer.

That said, somewhere beyond that dark and ominous cloud, beyond the silver lining, Tomás extends his hand to greet Angélica. Angélica extends her hand to greet Tomás. As they touch, at this very moment, the cornfields turn to shit. But it's OK, because the shit smells like roses.

¿Qué milagro? What miracle?

On To My Usual Place

I was walking to my usual place today. The sky was clear and I saw the moon in the daylight. I saw the moon in the daylight every day when I was a boy. I thought that everyone saw the moon.

Today, when I was walking to my usual place, I came across a man on the road. I said to him, "Look there, the moon is in the daylight."

The man on the road gave me a quizzical look and said, "That's a little puff of a cloud."

I smiled and said, "Oh yeah, the moon can be tricky. Did he trick you or did he trick me?"

The man gave me the same quizzical look and walked away, without saying a word.

So, I continued on to my usual place.

To Be Acquainted

A man from Louisiana, for contrary circumstances, came to reside in Redwing Minnesota. This poor man lived in a shack just outside of town with his wife and children. Not owning a horse, he walked into town to work as a smith's apprentice. Often he stayed for days to complete other odd jobs.

One winter day, he decided to walk home. It would have been prudent to stay in the warmth of the smith's shop. This day was bitterly cold, but his family was waiting and needed him. As he struggled through the deep snow, he realized that this was the kind of cold that could injure or even kill a man. He longed for the mild climate that he so enjoyed during his youth.

He fell into a daydream and found himself standing in a distant land. It was unlike anything he had ever seen. There were giant plants and trees. Strange animals moved about. Talking rocks murmured wantonly to the mountains. Beneath a beautiful blue sky, billowy clouds rolled playfully. This could have been heaven, he thought.

The ground rose up and cradled him, as if he were an infant. The Sun dropped from the sky and hovered like a mother peering into a crib. Drops of light fell like rain, filling the earth, creating a vast luminous ocean. The man floated there. The Sun spoke, "I was there, at the beginning, when the world was only water. A drop fell from a frozen star that passed too closely to my flames. Fire from my mane dipped into the water and gave a stir. From this ocean, *life* was born. If you, are alive Creole boy, then I am within you."

The Sun withdrew quickly and the Moon appeared. The Moon spoke, "I was there, at the beginning, when *new life* rose from the ocean depths. It was I who sent North Wind to give *new life* its first breath. If you, are alive Creole boy, then I am within you. Remember me and the cool North Wind, when your world has burst into flames."

To show his strength, Moon sent North Wind down. North Wind gave the man a slap, spinning him around.

The poor man woke from the daydream. He was nearly home and was no longer cold. He felt warm. He felt alive.

When the man arrived at his home, he told his family of this miracle. Many times, throughout his life, he retold the story. The tale, of how he became acquainted with Sun and Moon.

Wind and Tree

Playful Wind made a new friend. Wind said, as he breezed by, "Hey, Tree, come. Let's go for a walk."

Tree replied, "I'm a tree. I'm not a giraffe. I can't walk around because I have roots in the ground. Why don't you have a rest here in the shade of my branches?"

Wind didn't want to rest that day, so he continued to breeze about.

Later, Wind came back to Tree and was impatient, "Why won't you walk with me? I tell you what, I'll help you to walk."

Tree said, "No, I can't walk. I'm a tree." Wind didn't listen and he breezed through Tree's branches. At first, it was fun. Wind and Tree screamed and howled, "Weeee! Woooo! Yeah!"

But then, Wind began to push Tree harder and harder. Tree was no longer having fun. Tree was losing leaves and his branches felt like they would break.

"Stop!" said Tree. But Wind continued to push, harder and harder, until Tree had fallen. Tree's roots were pulled from the ground. Tree began to slowly die.

Wind said, "I'm sorry! I'm sorry!"

Tree said, "Sorry is too late. Sorry won't stand me up and fix my branches. We can be friends, but you have to accept me as I am."

Wind was sad and breezed away.

Tree later had a new life, as a kitchen table. And there was a dog that always asked Table to play outside.

One day Wind breezed by and said, "Hey, Dog, sit! I'd like to tell you a story about respecting your friends and accepting them as they are."

The Conditional Student

One day, a very novice student, decided to step outside the bounds of proper protocol and etiquette. He approached the Great Master with a question. "Master, please explain to me the essence of your fighting style?"

The Master thought to himself, "Who is this kid and didn't anyone explain chain of command to him?" But the master simply smiled and answered, "You *would* learn this *when* you learn this. In time, with patience, you *could* understand your own essence. But if you must know... If you are fire, I am water. If you are walking carelessly and unaware, I am banana peel. If you are a bad-ass mo-fo criminal type, then I am Starsky, Hutch, *and* T. J. Hooker."

The novice student was not fazed by the Master's profound assertions. The student, thinking himself clever, composed some other probing questions. "But Master, what if *I am* water? What if *I am* banana peel?

What if *I am*, whoever those guys are you mentioned? What then, are you?"

The Master appeared pleased with the young student's comeback and answered, "Well, then we would not be fighting. We would be a river flowing through an '80s sitcom. There would be a disco ball. 'Atomic Dog' would be bumpin' out my speakers. And we would then make sweet, sweet love."

The student was disturbed by the Master's words, and a little nauseated. He said nothing, turned, and quickly walked away.

The Master laughed and called out to the fleeing student, "I didn't want to answer your questions anyway. I was on my way to lunch. If you're not prepared to consider any possible answer, don't ask the question. And next time, follow the chain of command. Novice!"

I'm Not Lazy

I Just Don't Do Yard Work

This is kind of a roundabout way to explain something to my wife. She thinks that I'm just lazy. Not true! I'll do any other chore or housework, but I will not do yard work. This all goes back to a time before I ever met my wife. It was a whole other life.

I've heard many times on cable science programs that we are all made of stardust. And energy does not dissipate, it only changes. We all have some cosmic collective past.

In another life, it would have been hard for me to imagine this stardust thing. For me, life was controlled chaos. I was anxious and fearful. I constantly traveled. Even though I feared flying, I flew often for work. I won't say what kind of work. I will say that paranoia was crucial to my survival. I was *not* delusional.

Danger really did lurk around every corner. There were few times that I knew peace. They didn't last. I always had to go back to work.

I remember one peaceful time. I sat beneath a big tree in a small park. I sat very still. I breathed deep and imagined that I was the tree. It was amazing. My roots stretched deep into the earth. I drew up water. I was nourished by the soil. And the photosynthesis thing, wow! It's awesome! Honestly, I tried not to think about the carbon dioxide to oxygen conversion thing. When I did, I would hyperventilate. I did like my thick trunk and my many leaves.

I was so good at being a tree that squirrels climbed on me and played. Birds perched on my shoulders and sang. I preferred the squirrels though. The birds tended to poop on me. But it was all good. They were good company.

Unfortunately, I had to stop being a tree and get on a plane. I had responsibilities and duties. Since I was afraid to fly, I had the bright idea to pay for an extra seat and carry on a parachute. This was always a problem. Security would ask silly questions in serious tones. "Why do you need a parachute, sir? Is something going to happen to the plane?" Well, after a call to my "psychiatrist", my parachute and I would usually board.

Though, the last time I flew, my parachute was not allowed to board. Of course, *that* plane crashed. Anyway, good news, I came back, as a tree.

I lived as a real tree. No joke! As a tree, I didn't mind the carbon dioxide to oxygen conversion thing. I didn't mind the bird poop either. It was normal. I was a bird haven. And my roots were real. My leaves were plentiful like the stars in the night sky. I didn't have to *believe* I was stardust. I *was* stardust. I couldn't *be* without the sun, the rain, and the soil. I was comforted by the passing of time. The changing of the seasons was like a patient heartbeat. I lived peacefully as a tree for more than a century. I'm not sure what century though, being that I was a tree and all.

Then one day, I imagined that I was a man. Sure enough, a logger came along and cut me down. So here I am, a man once again.

Anyway, good news, I don't fear flying anymore. I fly as often as I can. And I never carry on a parachute. I just sit back, breathe deep, and imagine that I'm a tree. In case the plane crashes.

I now have a terrible fear of pretty much any gardening tool. So, I guess that makes me a garden-tool-a-phobic. I suppose in today's terms, it would be called garden tool anxiety disorder. It doesn't really matter. The point is, I DON'T DO YARD WORK.

So, sweetheart, I'm not lazy. I was terribly traumatized by a logger with a chainsaw.

Lighthouse Beacon

Lighthouse Beacon: *The First Flash*

John and Patricia Roth, and Michael and Gertrude Smith, sit enjoying the ambiance of their favorite restaurant. They are old friends. They share decades of memories. They also share righteous vindication. Chuckles can always be heard as they discuss their grown children's struggles with their own misbehaving, non-household chore doing, eye rolling, children. What a delight.

At their usual haunt, at their usual table, approaches their usual waiter. "Good evening. Mr. Roth, can I start you off with your *usual* before dinner?"

"No thanks."

The usual waiter pauses and looks surprised. He always assumed that with the Roths, his healthy gratuity depended on how toasty Mr. Roth got, by the end of his meal. Always best to get him started early. The Roths are usually easy to serve. Their dining experience reads like a well-rehearsed script.

So, the waiter adlibs, "*Not* the usual, something *unusual* then... Here is our wine list."

Mr. Roth stops him politely, "No thanks. Please give us a moment to look at the menu."

"Certainly."

The waiter walks away, baffled and worried about his tip. He can hear muffled, but lively chuckles from the table.

Laughing as he speaks, Mike says, "John, that kid looked like you just told him there was no Santa."

"No, I'm still Santa. I just don't plan on being so jolly tonight."

"So, you're *really* giving up booze?" asks Gertrude.

"Well Trudy, no choice."

Weeks before, doctors had passed some flexible surgical doohickey through what John calls, "unmentionable parts", straight to his heart. Guck was cleaned out, built up from years of... let's just say, "unhealthy living." All done without cutting open his chest. Oh, the marvels of modern medicine. What a delight.

Trudy leans in and looks John squarely in the face. This maneuver always precedes some serious query. As the digits in her age creep ever closer to the unknown instance of, yet certain occurrence of, death, Trudy finds religion with increasing zeal.

"John, Pat tells me that when you were on the operating table, they lost you for a few minutes. You basically died and came back. Did you see anything?"

"You mean, like a light, or something?"

"Yeah."

"Trudy, you always say God is everything."

"So, you saw God?"

"I saw *everything*, but I don't think it was God."

Lighthouse Beacon: *The Second Flash*

The FBI is struggling to understand the brutality; the blood, the rage. A double homicide... An elderly couple, both raped and tortured... So many questions... Why? How? Who could do such a thing?

No one sees them enter. One moment, no one is there. The next moment, is a nightmare.

The leader is an alpha-male type. He is six foot one, with dark hair, broad shoulders, and a strong back. He is fit and handsome. "Alpha" carries a smile that is at once charming *and* menacing. The eyes betray his need for control. If one could bear to stare into them, undoubtedly, his vicious nature would shine through.

The male accomplice is a crazed berserker, who thinks of himself as the muscle. In fact, his strength emanates from his feverish insanity. The idea was hatched in the damaged mind of his youth. But these deeds only came to pass when he encountered his partners.

"Berserker" is a true monster. He is little more than wrinkled, tattooed flesh, covering bones. Sunken eyes peer out from behind oddly pale, naturally blonde hair. A black leather vest and jeans contrast the dead appearance of Berserker's flesh. From high cheekbones to a narrow chin, his face is withdrawn and concave.

When he smiles, his lips draw back. Dimples convert into long deep pits, like parentheses; framing oversized mule teeth. Since childhood, Berserker has always assumed that Death was near and ready to take him. This thought is freeing. He has nothing to lose.

The female accomplice is withdrawn and timid in demeanor; seemingly submissive. She is always willing to stand by while Alpha and Berserker have their fun. She is patient. She kneels close by, sitting on her heels. Straight black hair, weighed down by oil from neglected hygiene, veils her face. She almost always leans forward with her head tilted toward the floor. Looking up, the hair is momentarily pulled back behind the ears; only to fall forward again, covering her face. She is slender and disheveled. Her mind is detached and distant; until some portentously abominable thought is triggered by who knows what. She rises up full of rage. In these times, Alpha and Berserker give her a wide berth. "Submissive" transforms and becomes the most dangerous of the evil trio. Her fury culminates in murderous bloodbaths.

Lighthouse Beacon: *The Third Flash*

"Patty?"

"Oh, John, you're home now. How was your walk? Got that old heart of yours pumping?"

"Yeah... what's going on?"

"Oh, I'm just straightening up. Our new loveseats came. The delivery man just left. You didn't see him? Tall, dark, and handsome fellow... Oh, and such a flirt..."

"He'll be back" John says solemnly.

With a smile, Patty placates, "Oh John, I was just kidding. You know you're my one and only tall, dark, and handsome."

Here's where two worlds collide. Alpha delivered two loveseats to John and Patricia Roth. In their skewed thinking, Submissive and Berserker believe home invasion is best done hiding within furniture. Such grim Trojan horses... Alpha quietly thinks they are both idiots. But, as long as they get the job done, he's OK with it.

Submissive and Berserker both share this thrill. They imagine themselves to be animated corpses; rising from their graves to terrorize the living. When the room is clear, they make their way free of the hidden spaces. Berserker unlocks the back door so Alpha can join them. "Son of a bitch, you forgot to take the plastic off again!" Alpha chuckles a little, as Berserker complains.

Alpha's initial thrill is when they are discovered in their victims' homes. The victims always hesitate, because they recognize him as the handsome delivery guy.

Patty comes to the threshold that leads into the living room. With a surprised look on her face, she asks, "What are you doing in my home?"

Before the evil trio can answer, John steps in and says, "They're here to kill us, dear; among other things." Not only is Patty shocked by her husband's words, but the evil trio is taken aback as well.

After a moment, Berserker speaks, "How do you know that, old man?"

"I saw everything."

"Everything?"

"Yeah, everything... I went to hell and I saw what you did. Everything..."

The trio bursts into laughter. Alpha adds, "I like you. This is gonna be fun."

Berserker asks, "Old man, what'd you go to hell for?"

John Roth smiles as he answers, "I kill three people."

John pulls a handgun from behind his back. The first flash from the gun's muzzle, looks to the trio as if it is far off in the distance. It appears as a lighthouse, warning ships to steer clear of a rocky coast. But this beacon flashes only twice more.

All goes dark. In the darkness, the trio sees everything. Everything becomes clear.

God, is everything, but not for them.

You Bastard!

This morning's berth to the conscious world is cold and frost covered. On a small island, on one of Canada's many lakes, beneath a canvas tent, lies a young man struggling to feel human. The previous day's portages were long and hard. His body pains in places that before seemed unknown to the human anatomy. The ground where he now stirs, seems as cold and rejecting as a young mother, whose unwanted newborn is left unattended and dying. Even colder and more numbing than when a steel blade meets flesh.

He steps from the tent. The gray cloud cover and gray reflected water, close in, boxing him, testing his senses. No longer is the water clear. No longer do crystal reflections dance in his eyes. Rather, plates of ice float and fog sits motionless in the middle of the lake. The fog looks like a great sailing ship, like that on which the ancient mariner rhymed. He stands at the edge of the lake. He sees the ship's skeleton faces leering. Looking again gives sight of a familiar face.

"You bastard!" he yells.

"You bastard!" says his echo.

"I loved her!" he yells.

"I loved her!" says his echo, playfully, like a child instigating and keeping count. But there is no real count. He is yelling at his own disgusting reflection.

"You bastard!"

Heartland

Somewhere... "Heartland" of America... Rural Indiana, maybe... I'm not sure. I can see myself, but I don't know who I am. There's no bliss in my ignorance. It's terrifying. It's a nightmare.

Heartland: part 1

Nothing's changed much since I left twenty years ago. I was a young boy then. Now during my return, reminiscence of my childhood rush upon me. Sights, sounds, smells... The monotonous landscape view of interstate highway "Heartland America" from my bus window... I'm sure nothing has changed much.

I remember the contrasting generalities of the town's diverse exactitudes. The smell of fertilizer on a hot mid-day, after a morning rain, met with the perfumed air of rose gardens in the town square.

I remember women in the church kitchen preparing the Sunday brunch. The smell of fried chicken and hot water cornbread made us forget stern monitions against gluttony. And there were various parts of pig, cooked in various ways. My father was fond of saying that Jesus was a man of the people; who preferred ham hocks.

Women dressed in their Sunday best. Men with broad smiles, proudly observed their offspring romping through the churchyard. Nothing's changed much; I'm sure.

Up the road, aways from our church, was the coloreds' church. I remember the lively praising hymns and boisterous sermons of the colored preacher Rev. James. The colored congregation could be heard over the distance.

Rev. James was a man who knew the Lord. No man dared say he didn't, not a colored or a white. There was the ever present fear of getting an impromptu sermon in the middle of anywhere, from a very large black man. Rev. James' righteous and adamant preaching style could put the fear of God in any man. Many times, just fear...

Well, that's the town I remembered. Festive on

Sundays, all about work during the week... But not this Sunday... I stepped off the bus and looked around. It was a wasteland. Apathy had come and built a new homestead on old land and tradition. The town was infected. The air smelled of sickness. There was tension with only two steps. I felt rejected and resisted against. The few people that were on the street, hurriedly went about their business. None looked up. I felt like getting on the bus and going back. But I stood there as the bus doors shut behind me, and it pulled away.

Nearby was Joan's diner. I would go there for malts and to play with Joan's daughter, Susan; on whom I had a crush. Sitting at a table in the diner, were two men, not speaking, but sharing a bowl of gruel. Neither looked up, but another man at the counter, looked directly at me. Deep in his weather-beaten face were set eyes which were much warmer than his smile. I realized that he was family, a cousin perhaps. I smiled back as I sat beside him at the counter. I placed my backpack on another stool. His clothes were grungy; matching the countertop, the floor, and all the tables. On the counter stood a bottle of scotch. It was half full or half empty. One of his tense hands clutched a glass. The other was a clinched fist, tight and laden with oil, dirt, and sweat. In total, he was a tense, unkempt, somewhat emaciated, deflated mess.

"Good to see you again" I said, knowing that he was indeed a cousin whose name eluded me.

"Yeah, it's good to see you too." He handed me a glass of scotch and upon his doing so, the other men promptly departed the diner. Being unsettled, I looked for small talk.

"Where're Joan and Susan?"

"They're gone."

"Whose diner is it now? Who runs the place?"

"This diner..." hesitating, he looked down at his scotch. Looking at me and then around the room, he said in a low voice, "This ain't a good place to talk. I'll get in touch with you. Take care of yourself."

He took his bottle of scotch and headed for the door. He acted as though he was being watched. I was certainly watching as he scurried up the street. I, left wondering, of what he was fearful.

Heartland: *part 2*

I walked through the town and everything was abandoned. The schools, the churches, and the shops were all closed. Only the boarding house had a light.

I walked in. "How much for a room?"

"You've got enough" said an old balding man behind the front desk. "Three floors, take any room. There's fresh linen and towels in the closets at the end of each hall. You can get the key tomorrow." He then walked away, disappearing into the room behind the front desk.

I followed his instructions and found a room on the second level in the front of the house. The room was pleasant and welcoming, considering all that I had seen that day. It was dusty, but in order. The furniture was in good condition. The wallpaper was faded. The drapes were so sun-bleached that the crossed pattern of the window panes had been imprinted. The window opened easily. Easily came a soothing breeze. And easily came sleep. It was now after sunset and a heaviness was upon me. I resolved to find my family and answers to my many questions in the morning.

The last thing I saw, as my eyes closed, was the chair in the corner of the room. It was illuminated by moonlight through the room's open window. This image lingered in my mind as I fell into sleep. It gradually changed. The chair became blurred. Slowly a new image came into focus. A colored boy sat facing me! He observed me. He studied me without expression, without malice or anxiety. I was terrified. I was shaking and confused. Smaller and smaller, I became. I felt helpless. Larger and larger, became the colored boy. More weighted was his eminent conclusion. I felt that he would come down on me with his hand and smash me into nonexistence. I twisted and turned and screamed. I wanted to wake up.

At this point, he disappeared, though I felt his presence. He had become a dark void, moving quicker than my eyes could follow. It moved to either side of me, hovered above, slid beneath, and then through me. I was exhausted. He was gone. It was gone. My mind went blank.

Heartland: *part 3*

The morning was difficult. I was fatigued. The sleep was too long, but not enough. My head hurt every way I turned. My eyelids were sore and didn't want to open. The morning sun only served to intensify my head pain. There was an emptiness rumbling inside of me. Considering the nightmare, I thought, "Oh my God! What's happened to me?" I then realized that I was merely hungry. Finding humor in this, I sat laughing in pang at myself. Now motivated, I got up to search for food.

No one was around. So I took it upon myself to enter the kitchen. There were no fresh foods. I found only canned fruits and vegetables, and drink mix packets. I made do. Again, I found humor. I said aloud, "This would be great, if I were pregnant." But no one was there to share my laughter.

Walking out into the town, I found it to be the same as the day before, bleak. There were a scarce few people. They watched me. I felt their many questions. I had no answers. My only response was to step lively past their inquisitive eyes.

The family farm was on the edge of the county. A few country paces more than what my city raised legs considered walking distance. There was no traffic. I had no choice, but to walk.

The trek led me through potholed town streets and down unpaved dirt roads. The farmhouses were dilapidated and covered by wild uncultivated vegetation.

Along the way, I found a strawberry patch. I also dug up sweet potatoes. It all fit nicely into my backpack, except for one sweet potato. I cut away the skin and dirt and ate it raw. I mused, "What a wonderful harvest Adam must have had in Eden."

Heartland: *part 4*

It was midafternoon when I reached the family farm. The old homestead was broken. All that was left of the happiness, woe-less comfort, and relative wealth, were delinquent hauntings. Trees stood in disarrayed sentry.

Boarded windows prevented me from looking inside, but I felt another heart beating. I searched for an opening and came across an unlocked cellar door. The door swung open as if I were expected. Emerging from the cellar was the cousin I had encountered at the diner. Not speaking, he motioned for me to follow.

I became intensely aware of the heat. It leapt several degrees a pace. Hell-bent on fiery destruction of all it encompassed. The air was like chalk in my lungs and my nostrils burned with every breath. My lips stung as if acids were excreted from my pores. Everything was blurred. My vision was a narrow tunnel. I could see only what was directly in front of me. "Cousin" was standing in the doorway of a large barn. I chose to believe that salvation from the searing heat was in that barn. I staggered forward.

Time moved at a pace relative to no marker. It moved any which way; forwards, backwards, and not at all. The distance was always one step further than one step taken. I closed my eyes to escape the anguish of attempted comprehension. My mind diverted to childhood memories. The camaraderie of boys in the club house, the thrill of skinny dipping, spying on the girls, Susan's pretty white smile, and... everything went black.

I opened my eyes. To my surprise, there was no sun. I was lying on the barn floor. An odd mixture of relief and turmoil was prevalent. The air was thick with a moist coolness. An oppressive stench reached out and grabbed me by the gut. Crouched in the shadows were small and large figures.

"You're OK" Cousin said, as he helped me to my feet. "You aint got the sickness. It's just your first time here an' you feel for these people. That means you got a sensitive heart. I hope it's a strong one too."

For several minutes I could not speak. My surroundings had thrown me into a terrible shock. "What is this place?" I managed to utter. Once again Cousin turned and walked without speaking. Once again, I followed.

My eyes were adjusting and what I saw went beyond shock. It was repulsion, and repulsion again at a new level. There were animals. Goats, cows, and pigs were penned by their necks to the floor. Some were bound together in twos and threes; immobilized by tight bindings of chain and rope. It was difficult to know how many were alive. Certainly, some were dead. The smell was unmistakable.

All around were crimson buckets. Hanging from a rafter above a horse stall, was a cow with a great many bloodied tubes protruding from its bruised flesh.

A few feet away were many human shapes huddled around a bucket. It was like a campfire, giving warm life on a cold winter night. In the center was a small girl, maybe four or five years old. Huge reflective owl-like eyes took up half her face. She had the squatting posture and nervous alertness of a circus monkey. She licked one hand while the other rested on the lip of the bucket. All the while she watched. When I moved, she reoriented and refocused. Her eyes lit up like fire. They flared when met with a fine beam of light, through the barn door. Startled, I stumbled backwards into Cousin's arms.

"What's in the buckets?" I asked.

"Blood" he replied.

"Fuck this! I'm outta here." I ran with accelerat-

ing pace. Feet moving in rapid succession... Uncon-
scious of effort... Like the swift directive flight of a
homing bird, retreating to the safety of familiar land...
Wham! On the ground once again... Knocked there by
the sunlight, thick and heavy like cast iron...

"You can't go yet. You've got to help us" Cousin
said.

"Help you? How? What the hell is this place?
What the hell is going on? Who the..."

Cousin shook me violently and said, "Calm
down! I'll explain everything!" I sat up, braced against
the barn wall, and listened.

"About fifteen years ago, strange things began to
happen. People began to disappear, mostly young boys
and girls. And weird animals were seen in the fields at
night. Then all the women folk took ill and many died.
They became very pale and their skin blistered from
the slightest ray of sunlight. They couldn't eat; especially solid or cooked foods. It came right back up. So
weak and thin, their only comforts were the dark and a
strange attraction to dying or freshly killed animals."

As Cousin was talking, in my mind I could see
Susan's young face. I remembered the malts and the
games of pretend and fanciful imaginings. All smiles

and laughter...

"What happened to Susan, Joan's daughter?" I asked.

"Susan died last year. That's her little girl back there by the stall. The children born after the sickness come, all have exaggerated features, especially the eyes."

"How did this happen?" I asked.

"Well, it all happened so quickly, less than a month. Many nights I couldn't sleep and when I did, I dreamed of the war. I'm a vet ya know!" he said with pride. "When I closed my eyes, I was there, on the battlefield. Artillery shells and flares, explosions and smoke, charred vehicles, and the smell of burning fuel and flesh... Guns raging overhead, crawling on my belly over dead soldiers, from both sides... But dead soldiers are all the same, just dead, no enemies. So when one day, all the men were gathering guns, I couldn't be a part of it. They said that the only people not affected, were the new folks that moved into the mansion by the lake."

Cousin continued, "That afternoon, excited and anxious, they headed for the old mansion. But that night they returned weaponless and beaten. Some were bleeding and moved about the streets slowly, like zombies. In their frustration, they chased the women and children out of town. Fleeing women and children settled here or at other barns on the outskirts of the county. At night they scavenge for berries, herbs, and flowers. They grind it all and mix it with water and blood."

As Cousin told this incredible tale, it occurred to me, I had not seen any women in town and there were virtually no men in the barn.

"Well, why didn't you get help from another town?" I asked.

"There's no telephones, or radios. That witch in the mansion controls the men in town. Some of the men not affected by her spells decided to go by foot to the next county. Some left by day, others by night. None were ever seen again."

"So what makes you think I can do anything?"

"You're our only hope" he said apologetically. "You're not from around here. You're unaffected. Maybe you can do it."

"I don't understand. Why can't you get on a bus and go to another town?"

"That's the thing; no bus has come to this town in fifteen years. You're supposed to be here, to help us. That's got to be it. Don't you see? Maybe you can do it."

"Do what?"

"Kill her."

Heartland: part 5

The mansion, with the lake as a backdrop, seemed like an oasis in a harsh desert. The grounds were lush, well-kept and orderly. Along the walkway were flowerbeds. Vibrant colors reached healthily toward the sun. Townsmen were coming in one hour intervals. I dared not leave my hiding place without the cover of night. So there I sat, some fifty yards from the place that Cousin only described as, "the witch's mansion." A witch, and I'm supposed to kill her?

As the sun was setting, the frequency and number of men increased. When the sun fell below the horizon, the flow of men abruptly stopped. I moved toward the mansion and could hear much revelry. Cautiously, I peeked through one window. I could see a huge orgy of food, gluttonous and excessive. There were fruits, large golden brown birds, a whole roasted pig with apple in mouth, fresh baked breads, wine, spicy sauces, and porridge. With great effort, I pulled away from the window.

The second window caused me no less hunger or longing. There was plush furniture, large pillows and cots all about, grandiose wall hangings, and a brilliant chandelier.

Some men were seated and others were re-clined. All eyes were indulgently fixed on the women in the room, shuttling about with food and drink. All of the women were uncommonly beautiful. Some had gener-ous features, luscious full lips and enticing broad hips. Smiling eyes sparkled like precious gems. Bountiful bosoms offered fulfillment and satisfaction. Fine silks, and shear cloth and lace were fashioned into little more than scant body wraps. Much was revealed. The young-er women were nimble wisps with strong contoured backs and long sleek legs. Breasts set high, supple and nubile. Erect nipples, pronounced and inviting. No doubt these women were soft, with juices flowing. I trembled at the thought. All these women bore odorif-erous fruits which caused some men to visibly salivate.

Upon entering the room, a fair young woman with a preciously girlish face, mischievous smile, and bright eyes, touched one man reclined on a pillow. He rose up and rocked in complimentary rhythm as she charmed him. She danced up and down his body. They swayed in unison. She touched him ever so softly. Her tools were delicate hands and strong callused feet. Nip-ples grazed his chest as she slipped a knee inside his fluid stance and slowly rubbed her thigh against his. Squaring up, she positioned her pelvis adjacent his and pulled them up close. Her body rippled and shook in an upward wave ending with a feathery kiss on his cheek. His body stiffened, eyes shut tightly as he fell back, supine, passive, and released.

Tears fell from my eyes and sweat on my brow. The heavy pounding of my heart was obscured by the pulsing of my swollen member. My lungs were choked. I fell to the ground, clutching myself. I passed out.

Heartland: part 6

Much time had elapsed, maybe hours. I was still on the ground beneath the window. I uncoiled and stretched my body out of the tucked fetal position I had assumed.

All the lights in the mansion were out. The window soundlessly swung open upon my touching it. Looking around, all was clear. So I climbed up and through the window. The instant my feet touched the floor, the lights came on. To my right a woman spoke, "Well, it's about time. I thought we'd have to send for you."

I must admit, the lights jolted me more than her voice. Her casual manner was certainly disarming. A feeling of surprise came over me. I had not fled, diving out the window perhaps. Even more surprising, I had no desire to do so. Was it a sense of purpose? Kill the witch! Save the town! Was I petrified or inspired? I still hadn't spoken or faced her.

Once again she spoke, "That's good. You are a thought-filled one. And you don't seem to be afraid."

I heard in her voice the significance of fear. Instinctively, I knew it was my trump. My survival depended on unflinching savvy and unblinking sophistication.

"You seem nervous though" she said.

"What makes you think that?"

"Well for starters, you came in through the window instead of the front door."

"I was being cautious."

"Of what?"

"I'm a thief of course." From this point she began to giggle. I continued without breaking stride. "When I was in thief school there was a saying, 'A rat almost never comes ambling in through the front door'."

Giggling, she said, "You look neither like a thief nor a rat."

I responded, "One of my teachers used to say, 'Black is passé. A thief should dress in a hospital gown. If caught, he can act lost and deranged, like an escaped mental patient'." This statement elicited more laughter.

"You're very refreshing, but not a thief. You're too nervous."

"Again, I am a thief and thieves are wary of front doors."

"Thieves are afraid of being caught. Wary, nervous, afraid, these are only words. What's the difference? I'd like to know how you really feel. The only muscles that you've moved are in your jaw. I know, why don't you turn and look at me. Of course, you're simply wary, not afraid."

Well, she got me there. "Fearless" I thought to myself and then turned to face her.

There she was, seated to my right, in a simple wood and wicker rocking chair; not looking particularly evil or witch-like. There was not a hint of force or manipulation. Her expression was like stepping from the shade into the sunlight, on a chill fall day. Her total countenance was easy and sweet. The only word that comes to mind is radiant. Radiant, like when a boy looks at his first sweetheart. Her face was framed by reddish-brown, shoulder length, wavy hair. She possessed the lightness and vital glow that I usually associate with newborns. At the same exact time, she was weathered and bogged down by the ages. Sort of like a cohort and an elder... She was so vibrant and magnetic.

In an attempt to quell the chaos welling within me, I said tentatively, as a child might, "I looked, can I go now?"

"You would leave so soon? After all, this party was thrown in your behalf."

"How's that? Why would you throw a party for me? You don't even know me."

"It was a welcoming party. You're new in town and new to our fellowship."

"Uh, OK. Thanks for the party. I have to go now."

"Please stay? I've been waiting for you. I've been so lonely."

"How can you bring yourself to speak the word lonely? You've got a house full of men and women in some kind of trance or something. And you expect me to believe that you were waiting for me! You witch!" Damn! Am I suicidal or what?

"You obviously think that I am evil or some kind of..."

"Are you a witch?"

"I'm just like anyone else. I want to be loved. And I'm asking that you please stay. I want you to love me."

"What a load of... Love you!? You can easily have

any man in town. Why would you want me?"

"I have *every* man in town! But they didn't keep their part of the bargain. They don't love me. They fear me. Why should I keep my part? So, I simply control and manipulate them. You, on the other hand, might be different."

"Thanks, but no…"

"Don't be rash. I can give you unimaginable pleasure, if you stand beside me. Pledge your love to me for all eternity. I can give you heaven, or if you desire it, hell. I'll show you." She took my hand and led me out of the mansion toward the lake. I had no will to resist. Maybe, I had a will to be taken.

Heartland: part 7

Nature's soft commotion was frozen in twilight. The lake was beautiful; dark and enchanting, like polished coal encrusted with diamonds.

She appeared larger than the lake. Looming over the water, she said, "All that you see before you, is yours, if you pledge yourself to me." Lifting her arms above her head, brought the dawn. She drew from the lake, first the sun and then the moon. Mist and steam from fire and water, were instantly crystallized by the moon's cold breeze. A high crystal gate materialized. Beyond the gate, what was water, became land. The night became day. Walking past the gate, I felt like a child. I was warm and safe, floating in the womb of nature.

The surface was pulled back. I could see the sun, the moon, the stars, and the earth at once. They were illuminated and moved in precise order.

I walked along streams of wine. I waded into the pools. I marveled at the bubbling springs, stemming from the ages. Intoxicating honey-milk dew on rose petals, lulled me away from my ego. Acre upon acre of fruit blossoms, filled my breath and wafted me into the sky. If bliss and ignorance are the same, then this was downright and utter stupidity. Then I heard her voice. I began to descend.

Aware of my senses, I felt pressure all around. Consciousness became a heavy and terrible oppression. Again, she asked for my loyalty. I wanted to go back into the sky. I almost agreed, but I couldn't speak. She understood my silence and said, "Then I'll show you more."

The fall began. That buoyant floating sensation changed to a ridiculous drop. Not the measured and paced acceleration of gravity, but instantaneous motion. I tried to pull my knees into my chest, to counter the sick feeling that I was breaking apart. My body was spreading thinner and thinner. My breath was taken away. The gusting winds created a vacuum, pulling my lungs up into my throat. The couple of gulps that I managed were like opening a breadbox filled with a billion lit matches. Deeper and deeper, I went. Darker and darker, I was. Everything was cut off.

With my eyes closed, my mind released. I could envision past the sea of smoke. The horizon line had the orange glow of fired coals on a moonless night. The sky had a rusty hazed look as light filtered through the smog. Heightened awareness breached the distance. The expansiveness of the orange horizon became a wall of fire pressed against my face.

Prodding against my back, was my collective past. It never diminished. It stayed with me, growing fat and clawing.

Boulders fell from above; tangible, acute, and absolute. Igneous locutions pounded my head.

My whole left side was numb and cold. At moments, this seemed a relief. At others, this only served to accentuate my pain. The contrast between extremes, each defining the other... To my right, were tall mountains. The peaks cut deep along the length of my body. Wind through the valleys sheared flesh down to bone. All things inward were exposed. This was more terrifying than any horror I could imagine.

My soul was like a giant scab, covering the fears and the hurt. Nothing was doctored. Wounds festered and were quietly forgotten. I cried then like a child. I thought, every day of my life offered a new pain, or old pains in new dressings. "When will I be anything other than a baby? I need so much. I'm so small."

A black cloud came from below and swallowed me as a giant amphibian might. A sticky appendage extended out and drew me in. Darkness enveloped.

Heartland: *part 8*

Snap... There I stood. Amazingly, I was whole. These surroundings startled me; like the sudden emergence from a deep trance preoccupation, extending into subway daydreams. Like waking to the press of rush hour crowds, making their way to the markets to sell goods and services. Masses moving to the rhythms of the foremen's drums... The smiles are fallacious. Gracious, even when the foreman straddles their backsides. That's exactly how I felt, helpless. I could understand nothing in this world.

All around were fire pits. The fires moved like ocean swells; crashing against the rocky firmament. But there was no ebb. There was endless flow.

The ground beneath me gave a low rumbling moan, as if reeling in some excruciating agony.

One standing around each pit, was what I could only think of as thugs; dressed from head to toe in white. They looked like a perverse choir with cone shaped hoods. As they prodded and poked with their long forks, I could see their fascination. There was a certain pained gleefulness. Enchantment with the fire caused their expressions to be twisted and macabre. I contemplated that the love of causing pain was a trap.

Their hatred, condemned them to an eternity of the same. The final realization of self... Their fires burned within.

In the pits were many human forms. It was a terrible sight. I could never be prepared for such a thing. I felt again like a terrified child, waiting for a guiding force to come and lead me away.

Hands reached out from the fire. Arms, shoulders, and faces appeared. The faces were cherry red, twisted, and blistered. Those poor wretches ensnared in pure pain and agony. Enveloped by fire for an eternity... The flames of Sinai descended... These souls, like the burning bush, are never consumed.

"Get back in there you pigs! That's where you belong! You whores!" It was obscene. One man reached through the surface of the flame and grasped for the edge of the pit. He was violently and vulgarly rebuffed. One of the thugs used his long fork to push the man deep into the center of the pit.

The man surfaced again and he indeed looked like a pig. His face was fat and bloated. Eyes swollen shut and nostrils flared disproportionately. The nose was pressed back. He was barely recognizable as human. In the center of his face were merely two gaping holes, surrounded by floppy singed flesh. He gasped and coughed and heaved. Molten rock spilled from his mouth. "Your mother eats fire in hell!" said one of the thugs. And again the obscenities continued. I turned my back on this scene and covered my ears.

What I then saw was possibly more incredible. I was confused. I saw Rev. James with his entire congregation behind him. All were impeccably dressed in their Sunday best. Some wore beautiful gold and purple robes. The whole church stood atop a low hill with a plateau. They were unaffected by the surroundings. The plateau was green and fertile, unlike the rocky ground around the pits. There was a natural light contrasting the orange of the fire-horizon. Rev. James was in a different reality. He was a vision into another world.

At the base of the hill, standing in opposition, was a group of thugs, yelling obscenities. They kicked and threw fire at the gathered congregation. But the thugs were drowned out by the Rev.'s stormy bellowing. The fire rolled off his robe the way rain might bead off a windowpane made of diamonds and gold.

My hands were still over my ears, but the Rev.'s voice was penetrating. The Rev.'s righteous locutions pounded my head. "The wage of sin is death. Sin in death is the complete absence of God. Manifestations of sin in the flesh are the burdens of a corrupted soul. The corrupted soul encapsulates the burdens of the flesh that is weak. Death in sin is the rebirth of flesh and soul, outside of the Kingdom. The soul outside of the Kingdom is gopher-wood, held beneath water, impelled to rise. As gopher-wood seeks the surface, the soul seeks God. The natural course of seeking God, is to be cleansed by fire. But brothers and sisters, I'm here to tell you that there is salvation yet. You don't have to seek for all eternity. You can be with God right now. This fire is of your own creation. You can change your destiny. It's not too late. Repent of your sins! Call upon the Lord! Accept Jesus as your savior! Repent!"

It seemed that he would continue on, forever. I managed to squeeze in thoughts of my own, "How excruciating, a fire and brimstone preacher, preaching about salvation, in hell... And if this is completely without God, could He hear us anyway? If not, then the Rev.'s spiel was a cruel, torturous, indecently cheesy treat offered in a rat trap. I cannot begin to imagine the torment of being trapped in a fire pit with a never-ending reminder of how simple it could have been to enter the Kingdom. Cruel..."

This all was too much. I felt that I was slipping, going insane. "Maybe I'm already insane. None of this is real. This is not happening. There's got to be a way out."

A hand extended out to me from a nearby pit. Looking down, I saw the twisted face of a woman. A familiarity drew me closer. When at the edge of the pit, she forced open her eyes. I saw past her bloated features. Her mouth dropped open as if to speak, but I heard nothing. A horrible sight... I knew it was Susan.

Dropping to my knees, I wept. Tears rolled down my face, blending into the sweat and soot. "Please God, make it stop! Enough! No more! I can't bear anymore!"

Heartland: *part 9*

My eyes were closed, but the change was obvious. Heat was replaced by cool moist air. The smell of sulfur and burning flesh had disappeared. Noticeably, Rev. James was absent. Yet, his voice echoed in memory, like marks left from tight bindings; cut away after many years.

I opened my eyes. I was back on the lake. In the distance I could see the crystal gate. The entire lake had become a crystal garden. Still on my knees, the garden was gorgeous in every detail.

I stood up, and was no longer beguiled. The flowers, the trees, everything was beautiful. But I saw them as fraudulent and artificial. They were like stage props.

The moon was ice, with a backdrop of deep blue-black. The moon's light filled the garden as if it were day. The only way to describe the contrast, is to say that, it was queer.

"I'm sorry to have put you through all of that" she said as she stepped from behind a tree. "I had to show you hell, so you could appreciate heaven." She was incandescent. Moonlight filtered through the crystal tree beside her. She spoke informally and was very apologetic. Her gentle tones and concern seemed absurd to me.

The approaching moments would be the crux of this ordeal. My time was near.

"Will you stay here with me? Will you love me?" Her words had additional meaning. The garment she wore was so sheer, that I wondered why she wore anything.

"Everything that you see is yours. Need you only to ask."

"There it is" I thought. That's the trick. She gains nothing by giving me everything. If I have everything, she has nothing; not even my love. She couldn't truly believe that I would love her. She doesn't intend to give me anything. It's all a lie. I would lose my soul for nothing. My faith would be in her, not myself or anything else.

I realized that this was her hell. Any man who is afraid of her, she would not want. And any man, who is not afraid, would not want her.

My long silence provoked her. "What say you!" she said archaically. I felt her force. Her face turned from soft radiance to a cold and determined glower.

The moon expanded behind her, filling the sky. It was surreal. The marble like surface, threatened to crush the garden.

I was unexpectedly happy and confident. These fantastical experiences had either pushed me to insanity or greatness. Perhaps the worst bringing out the best...

"There's not a lot to say" I responded. "You can't give me heaven and you can't give me hell. Salvation, redemption, forgiveness... these things are within me. I will choose my own destiny. To surrender my will to you, is to choose slavery. I cannot accept your offer, because there is nothing to accept."

Her face was now twisted and angry. She reeled in the anguish and dejection. "So be it!" she said and raised her arms.

In an instant the world changed again. It was dark and cold. I wondered if I was maybe in a dungeon, or a cave. Several minutes passed before realizing that I was not breathing. I knew then, I was at the bottom of the lake. I did not gag as much as I cringed. I thought to reach for the surface, but my bodily functions had already ceased. I was barely conscious. I couldn't move. I was trapped. Water filled my lungs and stomach. The cold was contrasted by the burning of regurgitated acids, flowing through my mouth and nose. The sensation was like being totally drunk, falling into a mound of biting ants, and being too weak to move away. Even this was fading. I was losing consciousness.

I thought of Rev. James and that the soul is gopher-wood. "I am impelled to rise." I wondered if this was my final destiny. I thought of Susan and Cousin, and the town. And I'm sure nothing has changed.

I remember the contrasting generalities of the town's diverse exactitudes. The smell of fertilizer on a hot mid-day, after a morning rain, met with the perfumed air of rose gardens in the town square. I'm sure nothing has changed.

Heartland: *part 10*

I faded, completely. Nothing was left.

I didn't know who I was. There was no bliss in my ignorance. It was terrifying. It was a nightmare.

I woke the next morning. I sat up. I cradled my face with my hands. I shook in amazed disbelief. I could think of only four things. It felt good to be alive... pen... paper... and... "Damn! I'm late for work."

A Beautiful Night For A Sleepwalk...
With Sunglasses

Engaged detachment
Thoughtful indifference
The excitement of melancholy
Dis-condition of ease
Disorder of the day
How passé?
Mania
How mundane?
Polar juxtaposition
Ask a physician
Ask the media
Ask for pills
Script is paid
Delirious trimmers
Sleep aids
Maybe sleep
Counting sheep
Counting toes
Left eye closed
Always sees
Dis-condition of Ease
Sleepwalking
Sunglasses
One eye open
Paranoid right
Beautiful night

Thank you for reading
The Dis-condition of Ease.
Look for a new title in 2019.
Sincerely,

Owen Patterson

www.ingramcontent.com/pod-product-compliance
Lightning Source LLC
Chambersburg PA
CBHW071324130626
46556CB00004B/1732